LITTLE ONE'S SLEEPYTIME TALES

ILLUSTRATED BY
PAMELA STOREY AND ERIC KINCAID

BRIMAX BOOKS · NEWMARKET · ENGLAND

THIS BOOK BELONGS TO

Heather McKeown

CONTENTS

Page

A Tug of War
Traditional   9

The Little Truck that made the Town Jump
by Robert Moss   16

The Gingerbread Man
Traditional   22

Rimski and the Weather-Vane
by Rosalind Sutton   26

The Three Wishes
Traditional   32

Little Red Hen
Traditional   39

Pip the Pup
by Robert Moss   42

Jonathan John has a Lazy Day
Traditional   48

The Magic Pot
Traditional   55

The Yellow Paint Pot
by Lucy Kincaid   60

The King of Birds
Traditional   66

A Singing Lesson
by Lucy Kincaid   72

Humpty Dumpty
by Rosalind Sutton   78

Bedtime
by Thomas Hood   80

ISBN 0 86112 294 1
© BRIMAX RIGHTS LTD 1985. All rights reserved
Published by BRIMAX BOOKS, Newmarket, England 1985
These stories and illustrations are also published in
a collected edition 'A Book of Dreamland Stories'.
Printed in Belgium

A Tug-O-War

All was peaceful in the forest. The birds were singing, animals were grazing, butterflies were flitting, Mother Sparrow was sitting on her nest waiting for Father Sparrow to bring her a worm. Father Sparrow was at the waterhole.

"Move over Mr. Crocodile," he said. "I want to drink."

Mr. Crocodile opened one lazy eye. "If I want to lay in the waterhole, then I will," he said. "Go and find a drink somewhere else."

Father Sparrow was cross, but how can a sparrow argue with a crocodile?

He found a worm and took it to Mother Sparrow. He was sitting in the tree beside her when there was a tremendous bump. The tree shook and trembled as though it was about to fall.

"What's happening?" chirped Mother Sparrow anxiously. If the tree fell, their nest would fall too and her eggs would break.

"It's Mr. Elephant," said Father Sparrow. "Hey there Mr. Elephant, why don't you look where you are going? You nearly shook our nest from the tree."

Mr. Elephant said nothing.

"You might say you are sorry," said Father Sparrow.

"I might, but I'm not going to," said Mr. Elephant.

Father Sparrow was very annoyed at his rudeness. "I'll tie you up if you dare to do it again," he said.

Mr. Elephant laughed. "YOU tie ME up, ha . . . ha . . ." and he plodded off into the forest rumbling and gurgling with laughter.

"Just you wait and see," said Father Sparrow. He flew down to the waterhole. Mr. Crocodile was still bathing and he still would not let anyone near enough to get a drink. "If you don't come out of there I'll tie you up," said Father Sparrow.

"You might tie me, but you'll never hold me," laughed Mr. Crocodile.

"We shall see," said Father Sparrow and went in search of an extra long, extra strong vine.

The next time Mr. Elephant passed by the tree in which the sparrows had their nest, he bumped into it deliberately.

"Oh . . . oh . . ." cheeped Mother Sparrow.

"I'm going to tie you up," said Father Sparrow sternly.

"You might tie me, but you'll never hold me," laughed Mr. Elephant. And just to show that he wasn't afraid, he stood still and let Father Sparrow fly over his back and under his tummy with the vine and tie it in a knot.

"I will prove I can hold you," said Father Sparrow. "Just give me time to pick up the other end of the vine. It's behind that tree." While Mr. Elephant was still laughing, Father Sparrow flew to the waterhole with the other end of the vine in his beak.

"I'm going to tie you up AND I'm going to hold you," he said to Mr. Crocodile.

Mr. Crocodile was so amused, he left the water and came out onto the bank. "Go on then," he said, and waited while Father Sparrow tied the vine around his tail.

"Just give me time to pick up the other end of the vine," said Father Sparrow. "It's behind that tree."

Father Sparrow hid in the trees, and then called loudly, "Start pulling . . . NOW!"

Mr. Elephant began to pull. Mr. Crocodile began to pull. They both thought they were pulling Father Sparrow. Instead they were pulling each other. How they grunted and puffed!

"That sparrow is incredibly strong," grunted Mr. Elephant.

"That sparrow must be the strongest bird in the world," puffed Mr. Crocodile.

Mr. Crocodile and Mr. Elephant were very well matched. Neither one could move the other.

At sundown, Father Sparrow called from his hiding place.
"Are you ready to give in?"

"Yes . . . yes . . ." puffed Mr. Elephant. He was so tired.
He couldn't understand why Father Sparrow sounded so
fresh.

"Are you ready to give in?" called Father Sparrow again.

"Yes . . . yes . . ." grunted Mr. Crocodile. He was as tired
as Mr. Elephant. And he felt just as foolish.

"I'm letting go of the vine . . . NOW!" called Father Sparrow. And as he said "NOW" he cut it through the middle. Mr. Elephant lost his balance at one end and sat down with a bump. Mr. Crocodile lost his balance at the other end and slipped on the mud. They both disappeared into the forest with the sound of laughter ringing in their ears. It would be a long time before either of them were rude to Father Sparrow again!

The Little Truck That Made The Town Jump

Dinky was a little truck who worked for Sam Jones, the builder, and he was very unhappy. Every day for weeks he had been doing the same journey—carrying bricks and sand and cement and pipes and timber to where Sam Jones and his men were building a new school.

Dinky liked working for Sam Jones, who was a big, jolly man with a loud, friendly voice. Dinky loved rushing to and from Sam Jones's builder's yard with the things the men wanted for building. He didn't even mind doing the same journey there and back every day. The trouble was that on this journey to the new school he had to go so slowly. In fact, he almost had to crawl.

Dinky was a smart truck. He was painted blue with yellow stripes, and all his metalwork gleamed like silver and sparkled in the sunlight. And he could go really fast.

He was the fastest of all Sam Jones's trucks and vans, and he loved speeding along the road, humming merrily. When he carried a loose load he had great fun listening to it going bumpety-bump-thud-bumpety-bump-thud behind him, just as if it was beating time to the music of his engine!

But there was no fun at all on this slow journey to the new school, for there was a big, rude truck that went along the road at the same time as he did every day, and it stayed right in front of him, in the middle of the road, and wouldn't let him pass.

Once, Dinky tried to rush past the big truck, thinking it would move to one side of the road; but it didn't. Dinky's brakes had to go on sharply or he would have had to swerve on to the grass and he might have ended up in the ditch alongside.

After that, Dinky just had to rumble slowly along behind the big truck. He was most unhappy about it.

Then one day an astonishing thing happened. On being driven out of the shed where all Sam Jones's vans and trucks were kept, Dinky was loaded up with something big and heavy that he'd never seen before. It wasn't a boiler or a concrete mixer or a kitchen range. He couldn't see it very well, and he didn't know what it was. Dinky hurried out on to the road, but just as he began to get up speed, there, just in front of him, loomed up the big, rude truck.

"Honk, honk! Toot, toot!" Dinky's hooter blared out, but the big, rude truck took no notice; he just rumbled on, taking up most of the road and giving Dinky no room at all to pass.

Dinky was so eager to go faster that he gave a jerky kind of leap forward. The jerk broke the rope that kept the thing behind firmly tied up, and a sudden loud noise clanged out behind. It was so loud that Dinky jumped, and the big, rude truck jumped; the whole town jumped. CLANG, CLANG, CLANG!

"My word!" cried Sam Jones. "The school bell's broken loose!"

Then Dinky knew what it was he was carrying behind. It was a great big bell for the new school! It made a tremendous noise, and once it started clanging it kept on! CLANG, CLANG, CLANG!

The big, rude truck was so startled that it swung across the road, bumped into a lamp-post and came to a sudden stop.

Dinky rushed past. All the people on the pavements stopped to stare as he rushed on with the bell clanging loudly behind him. They thought he was a fire-engine! Shopkeepers hurried out of their shops to see what was happening. Dogs barked. Children shouted and cheered, and a policeman on point duty held up all the traffic. CLANG, CLANG, CLANG!

Dinky had never enjoyed anything so much in his life. He was excited "I'm a fire-engine!" he shouted, and raced on with the bell clanging out behind him. What a noise it made! People put their fingers in their ears so that they would not hear it. And it didn't stop clanging till Dinky came to the place where the new school was nearly built.

Sam Jones told all the men building the school what had happened, and he laughed and laughed, and they laughed and laughed, and everybody was pleased about it, though nobody quite so much as Dinky. He'd had a wonderful morning. He'd taught the big, rude truck a lesson and he'd made the whole town jump!

The Gingerbread Man

A little old man and a little old woman lived in a tiny cottage. Every day was the same because they had no children to play with or to make them laugh.

One day, the little old woman had an idea. It was such a splendid idea, she had to sit down and think about it. The little old man was sitting outside in the sun, so the little old woman said to herself, "I will make a little gingerbread man!"

She started mixing things, fat, sugar and eggs; then flour and ginger. She put in lots of ginger and made him a lovely dark brown. She rolled the dough and cut out the shape of a little man.

"Now, currants for his eyes and his buttons. Some lemon peel for his nose and his mouth . . . That's fine!"

She slid the gingerbread onto a baking sheet and put it into the oven to bake.

Later that morning, the little old woman heard a voice.

"Let me out! . . . Let me out!"

The voice came from the oven! Very carefully, she peeped inside. The Gingerbread Man leapt out!

"Wait!" she called. "Come back!" But he was off and running fast.

"Don't just sit there, little old man!" she cried. "Help me catch him!"

They ran after him.

"Stop! . . . Stop!" they shouted.

The Gingerbread Man grinned and called,

"Run, run as fast as you can

You can't catch me

I'm the Gingerbread Man."

And they couldn't!

A cow stood across his path. The Gingerbread Man ran between its legs.

"Mmm-ind your manners!" she mooed. "What are you doing?"

"I am running away!" laughed Gingerbread Man. "I have run away from the little old woman and the little old man, so I am running away from you!

Run, run as fast as you can

You can't catch me

I'm the Gingerbread Man."

He was right. The cow could not catch him!

He raced past a horse trotting through a gate.
"Whoa!" called the horse. "Wait for me!"
Are you running away too?" cried the Gingerbread Man.
"Why not? . . Hee-hee-ee!" neighed the horse. "The gate's open."
"I run away from everybody!" said the Gingerbread Man. "I will run away from you too!

    Run, run as fast as you can
    You can't catch me
    I'm the Gingerbread Man."

And even at a gallop the horse couldn't catch him.
Round the next bend he met a fox.
"Hallo!" called the fox. "Why, you are brown, just like me . . . Look, we make a good pair."
The Gingerbread Man didn't stop. He ran faster and faster, calling out, "I've run away from the little old woman, the little old man, a cow AND a horse, so I can run away from you!

    Run, run as fast as you can
    You can't catch me
    I'm the Gingerbread Man."

But . . . At last he stopped on the edge of a river.
"Oh!" said the Gingerbread Man. "I shall get wet . . . What can I do?"

Up came the fox.

"You can sit on my tail, little brown friend. We will cross the river in no time."

So the Gingerbread Man climbed onto the fox's tail.

Soon the fox said, "Little friend, you will get wet on my tail. Jump on my back."

So the Gingerbread Man jumped onto the fox's back.

Half-way across the river the fox said, "Little friend, you are too heavy. Jump on my nose . . . You will be able to see better."

The Gingerbread Man laughed and jumped onto the fox's nose.

"This is fun!" he said.

When the fox had nearly reached the other side, he tossed his head. Up went the Gingerbread Man, spinning over and over in the air. Then . . . snap! snap! He was caught!

The fox gobbled him up and that was the end of the Gingerbread Man.

Rimski And The Weather-Vane

Rimski was a young rooster. He had golden feathers round his neck, tail feathers of shining green and a croaky voice which grew stronger every day. Each morning very early, he flapped up on to the yard gate. There he stretched his neck and his wings, trying out his 'Cock-a-doodle-doo!' . . . Yes, it was improving—reaching a high note.

After he had crowed, he stopped to listen, hoping someone would answer him.

One morning from a long way away came a faint 'Cock-a-doodle-doo!' That was a great day for Rimski. He strutted about feeling very proud.

One day, as he made his first crow, the church clock chimed. He hadn't noticed it before—it had just been mended. The sound annoyed him. It spoilt his own wonderful sound. Lifting his head to see where the strange sound had come from, he saw something shining at the top of the church spire. Then he looked again—and again! Was it possible?

A bird up there? . . . Yes, a golden one! . . . What did it mean by singing out that silly 'Ding-dong, ding-dong' rubbish! Why couldn't it give a proper 'Cock-a-doodle-doo'? This was serious. The matter needed his careful attention.

Pulling himself up tall, Rimski let out a loud and long 'Cock-a-doodle-doo!' He gave his feathers a shake, as if to say, "That should fix him!" . . . There was no answer. "Ha!" said Rimski. "He can't beat that!"

27

Later, the chimes went again, to be followed by 'Dong, dong, dong, dong, dongngng!' Rimski was very angry. It bothered him. What could he do? He couldn't sleep that night and through the hours he heard its chimes and its dongs. By morning he had made up his mind.

He'd go and see him—this 'Ding-dong Goldie' as he had nicknamed him. HE would make him change his tune!

Up on the gate, then out into the lane—Rimski strutted off. Mrs. Tabby Cat saw him as she sat washing herself.

"Good morning!" she called. "Going somewhere?"

"Of course!" answered Rimski. "I have important business to attend to. That bird up there—I'm going to put him in his place!" He tossed his head towards the church spire.

Mrs. Tabby glanced up: "That IS his place!" she said . . . Rimski ignored her.

Presently he came to a donkey, tethered on the grass.

"Hee-haw!" cried the donkey. "Could you please undo this rope? . . . I'd love to come for a walk!"

Rimski didn't even stop. "Sorry! I'm off to teach that bird a lesson!" . . .

"Which bird?" asked the donkey.

Once again Rimski tossed his head towards the church.

"Oh, he only does what the wind tells him," said the donkey.

"He'll do what I tell him!" boasted Rimski.

In the churchyard, he perched on a stone to give a loud 'Cock-a-doodle-doo!' No one answered.

Mrs. Blackbird came, searching for worms, then stopped to chat. Rimski explained why he had come; but she found it puzzling that he should want to quarrel with the weather-vane!

When the clock chimed again, Rimski was furious. "There, listen! I'll stop him—this weather-vane!"

Mrs. Blackbird said he would have to go up because weather-vanes never came down.

"How?" he asked.

"You could fly," she suggested. But Rimski made excuses so she took him to the steps. Up and up! Round and round! "Keep going!" she called. His head spun!

At last he came to a wide platform. The clock whirred—then blared out. Poor Rimski! It was terrifying! He found the workman's ladder fixed to the spire. Holding with his beak, he went up slowly. There was the bird. Golden? Yes: but no bird—just a metal shape. It swung round flinging Rimski off—far out into space.

He flapped and flapped! The ground looked miles away—then nearer and nearer! He was going to crash! A strong wind lifted him just in time. As it was, he flopped down—pitching on to his nose.

Mrs. Blackbird cheered him up. "What a flight, sir! You'll be famous!"

Rimski felt better. "Thank you, madam. I can certainly tell the world about Goldie up there. He's not real—only a painted thing going round and round!"

Mrs. Blackbird laughed. "Whichever way the wind blows, I suppose. HE can't make the sounds then! Could they come from the clock, d'you think!"

Rimski considered. "Possibly! . . . Possibly! Yes, you can take it from me—they came from the clock."

Mrs. Blackbird went on, "If we counted each dong would that tell us the time?"

Rimski tried to think. He couldn't keep up with this clever blackbird. The clock struck.

"Gracious!" she cried. "I must be off! Goodbye!"

Rimski stared after her, gave himself a shake and started for home.

The donkey asked how he'd got on. "Fine!" said Rimski. "That bird is just a weather-vane turning in the wind!" The donkey laughed.

Mrs. Tabby Cat opened one eye. "Anything exciting happen?" she asked.

"Of course!" he replied. "I climbed the spire, checked the clock and the weather-vane, then flew down!" . . . He flapped on to his gate. 'The cat's right!' he thought. Stretching up, Rimski gave his very best 'Cock-a-doodle-doo!'

The Three Wishes

One cold winter evening, a woodcutter and his wife were sitting in front of the fire warming their toes. They were very poor and one of their favourite ways of passing the time on a cold night was to wish for things they did not have.

"You may wish first tonight," said the woodcutter's wife.

"I wish I had a pair of thick woollen socks to keep my toes warm," said the woodcutter, drawing even closer to the fire.

"I wish I had a fine woollen shawl to drape round my shoulders," said his wife.

"I wish I had a dappled horse to ride."

"I wish I had a dress of patterned silk."

I wish . . . I wish . . . The more the woodcutter and his wife wished, the sillier were the things they wished for.

"I wish I had a golden nail to mend the broken chair with."

"I wish I had a golden needle to darn your socks with."

"I wish I had a flying pig."

"I wish I had a singing duck."

But more than anything else they wished to be rich, to have all the things their neighbours had.

"If only our wishes would come true," sighed the woodcutter's wife. She and the woodcutter both knew that wishes do not come true, except in fairy tales.

Suddenly, a gust of wind blew the cottage door open with a bang. The door rattled and shook on its hinges. The woodcutter jumped up to close it.

"Wife . . ." he said, "we have a visitor. Fetch a chair."

"Come in . . ." he said, to the little person standing on the doorstep. "Come in and warm yourself by the fire."

"I have not come to stay . . ." said the fairy, for the stranger standing on their doorstep was indeed a fairy. "I have come to grant you and your wife three wishes."

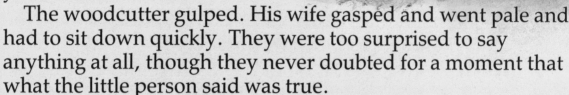

The woodcutter gulped. His wife gasped and went pale and had to sit down quickly. They were too surprised to say anything at all, though they never doubted for a moment that what the little person said was true.

"You have three wishes only," said the fairy, "so think well before you wish." And with that she was gone, as suddenly as she had come, and the door closed after her in another gust of wind and with another bang.

"Would you believe that . . ." gasped the woodcutter's wife when she found her voice again. "Three wishes . . . I wish . . . I wish . . ." The woodcutter quickly put his hand over her mouth.

"Stop!" he said. "Remember what the fairy said. We have only three wishes. We must not waste them."

"You are right, of course," said his wife. "We will both think hard and we will make our wishes tomorrow evening when we are warming our toes in front of the fire."

Neither of them slept well that night. Neither of them worked very well the next day. They were both far too busy thinking. There was so much they could have, if only they used the right words when making their wishes.

The next evening, the woodcutter's wife made up the fire, then she and her husband pulled up their chairs and got ready to make the wishes that were going to change their lives.

The woodcutter's wife leant forward and poked at the glowing logs. "The fire is burning well tonight," she said. And then without realising what she was saying, she added,

"I wish we had a nice big sausage to cook on it." You can guess what happened, can't you? Her wish was granted. She had a sausage.

The woodcutter was SO angry. "You have wasted a wish," he shouted, shaking his fist. "I wish that stupid sausage was growing on the end of your nose." And THAT was the second wish gone. If you have ever seen anyone with a sausage growing on the end of his or her nose, you will know how silly it looks.

The woodcutter's wife sobbed and sobbed.

"What shall I do . . . what shall I do . . ?"

"Hold still and I will pull it off," said the woodcutter. But it was a magic sausage and he couldn't pull it off. He couldn't cut it off either.

His poor wife buried her face and her long sausage nose in her apron and sobbed and sobbed. The woodcutter patted her shoulder.

"There . . . there . . ." he said. "Don't cry . . . we still have one wish left. We can still be rich. I will buy you a gold case to put round the sausage. That will hide it."

The woodcutter's wife wailed even louder at his words.

"I don't want a golden case round my nose. Everyone will laugh at me. Oh . . . there never was anyone more unhappy than I."

"You won't be unhappy when you are rich," said her husband.

"You can be rich if you want," sobbed the woodcutter's wife, "but I am going to run away to the end of the world and no one will ever see me, or my nose again."

"Please don't do that," cried the woodcutter. He caught hold of her arm and would not let her through the door. "We have one wish left. The wish is yours. Wish for whatever YOU want."

"I wish . . . oh how I wish . . . that the sausage would go from the end of my nose," cried his wife.

And THAT was the third, and final, wish. The sausage was gone. Though no one knows where it went. There were no wishes left and so the woodcutter and his wife stayed poor. They never saw the fairy again. No one ever heard them wish for anything ever again, even in fun, and in time they learned to be content with what they had.

Little Red

"My wheat
"Will you he
"Not too
"Don't
never d
"Yo
pigle

Little Red Hen strutted out of the farmyard and into Farmer Brown's big field. The wheat had been cut and gathered so she could scratch about anywhere.

"I might find some ears of wheat that the farmer's men have dropped," she clucked.

And she did. They were fine fat ones, full of golden grains. She carried them back to the farmyard to show her friends.

"Cluck, cluck!" called Little Red Hen. "Will you help me plant these grains?"

"Oh, No-o-!" yawned Ginger Cat. "I'm too sleee-py." Ginger Cat went up on to the roof of the barn and went to sleep.

"Oh, No-o-!" squeaked Grey Rat. "I am busy storing winter food in the barn." Grey Rat scampered away.

"Oh, No-o!" grunted Pink Pig. "I am off to find some acorns." She trotted away into the trees.

"Very well," said Little Red Hen. "I will plant them myself."

And she did. She put them in fine straight rows. She watched the rows every day. She saw green shoots peeping up out of the ground. Then she saw the wheat at the top begin to ripen in the sunshine. Little Red Hen was pleased.

"...is ready!" called Little Red Hen to the animals. "...elp me gather it?"

"...ay," said Ginger Cat. "I must wash my fur."

"...count on me," squeaked Grey Rat. "My work is ...one."

"...u can see I'm too busy," grunted Pink Pig. "I have ten ...ets to feed!"

"Very well," said Little Red Hen. "I will gather it myself."

And she did. She snipped each stalk and made a neat bundle.

"That's done!" she clucked. "Will you help me carry the wheat to the miller? The miller will grind it into flour."

"Impossible!" said Ginger Cat, opening one eye.

"Quite impossible!" squeaked Grey Rat.

"Quite, quite impossible!" grunted Pink Pig.

"Very well," said Little Red Hen, "I will carry it myself."

And she did. She carried it all the way to the mill. The great stones at the mill turned round and round, grinding the grain into flour. When the flour was fine enough, the miller put it into a linen bag.

"Thank you," said Little Red Hen.

When she came back to the farmyard, Little Red Hen called out, "Here is the flour . . . Who will help me take it to the baker to be made into bread?"

"Out of the question," said Ginger Cat, walking away.

"Quite out of the question," squeaked Grey Rat, running off.

"Quite, quite out of the question," grunted Pink Pig. "I am too fat to go anywhere."

"I suppose 'out of the question' means 'No'," said Little Red Hen. "I will take it myself."

And she did. She went to the baker and brought back a crusty loaf.

"Who will help me eat this lovely new bread?" she clucked. The animals all gathered around.

"I will!" said Ginger Cat, twitching his whiskers.

"So will I!" squeaked Grey Rat. "I am so hungry."

"Don't forget me!" grunted Pink Pig. "It looks delicious!"

"It is delicious," said Little Red Hen, "but you didn't help me at all . . . so it is quite out of the question for you to have any of it! Cluck! Cluck!"

Pip The Pup

Pip the Pup trotted out into the garden and sniffed the sweet morning air. He was feeling ready for anything. He looked this way and that way and behind him. And then he saw his tail. It stopped wagging as soon as he looked at it.

He looked at it with one eye for a time. He couldn't make up his mind whether it belonged to him or whether it was something that followed him about.

Pip was only a baby puppy, and there were lots of things he wasn't sure about. The tail was one of them.

The tail didn't move or make a sound. Pip gave a sharp bark at it to warn it that he had got his eye on it and it must not try any tricks on him.

Then he went on his way, growling loudly to show anybody who happened to be about that he was a dangerous fellow.

A sparrow hopped on to the lawn. Pip made a dash at it, but tripped and fell nose-first into a flower-bed. The sparrow went on hopping around just as if Pip wasn't there, so Pip barked furiously to show he wasn't a dog to be ignored.

Then he stopped and listened. Somebody was barking back! "Wuff, wuff, wuff!" barked Pip sharply. Then he cocked his head on one side and listened. "Wuff, wuff, wuff!"

He was right! Someone was answering him. Another dog! Off down the garden path dashed Pip, through the gate and into the lane. He just fancied a jolly romp with a dog friend. But which was the way to take?

Pip hesitated, not certain whether to go up or down the lane or over the meadow. Then he saw Harry the Horse trotting towards him down the lane.

"Excuse me," he said politely, "but do you know where another dog lives around here?"

"There are no dogs round here," snorted Harry. "You're the only dog, and you're not really a dog—yet. Good day!"

Harry splashed through a puddle in the lane and went on his way. Pip went thoughtfully over to the puddle and had a drink. Then he sat down in it and had a think.

Just then, Mrs. Penny Pig came bustling down the lane, followed by all her eight piglets, in single file.

"Oh, good morning, Mrs. Pig," said Pip. "Please can you tell me where another dog lives round here?"

"ANOTHER dog?" Mrs. Pig grunted. "What do you mean, ANOTHER dog? There aren't any dogs round here, and I hope there never will be."

"But I suppose," she added, looking sharply at Pip with her beady eyes, "I suppose YOU will be a dog some day. Come along, piglets, or we shall be late for market."

She hurried off, with her eight piglets squealing to each other behind her.

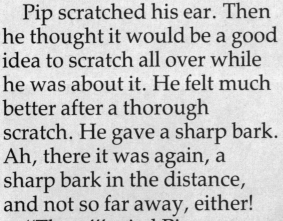

Pip scratched his ear. Then he thought it would be a good idea to scratch all over while he was about it. He felt much better after a thorough scratch. He gave a sharp bark. Ah, there it was again, a sharp bark in the distance, and not so far away, either!

"There!" cried Pip delightedly. "I wasn't mistaken. Wuff, wuff, wuff!"

"Wuff, wuff, wuff!" came the answering bark again.

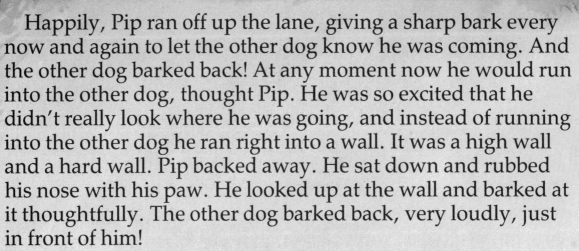

Happily, Pip ran off up the lane, giving a sharp bark every now and again to let the other dog know he was coming. And the other dog barked back! At any moment now he would run into the other dog, thought Pip. He was so excited that he didn't really look where he was going, and instead of running into the other dog he ran right into a wall. It was a high wall and a hard wall. Pip backed away. He sat down and rubbed his nose with his paw. He looked up at the wall and barked at it thoughtfully. The other dog barked back, very loudly, just in front of him!

"Why," cried Pip, "the other dog's there, just on the other side of the wall. Wuff, wuff, wuff!"

At that moment, there was a rustling and a stirring high up in a tree close by. The enormous eyes of Mrs. Owl peered down at Pip. "Whatever is the meaning of this dreadful noise?" she scolded. "Don't you know I go to sleep during the day? How dare you make such a disturbance!"

"Oh, dear!" said Pip, "I'm very sorry, Mrs. Owl. I forgot you would be in bed. I was just saying hello to the other dog behind the wall."

"Other dog? What other dog?" said Mrs. Owl. "There's no dog behind the wall, or in front of it, either," she added, peering down at the baby puppy, "because YOU can hardly be called a dog."

"There is a dog," said Pip. "Listen! You can hear him bark at me. Wuff, wuff, wuff!"

"Wuff, wuff, wuff!" came back to him. "There! Did you hear?" cried Pip.

"You silly, stupid, noisy puppy!" cried Mrs. Owl crossly. "That is not another dog. It's YOU. It's your own bark coming back to you from the wall—an echo!"

Oh, dear! Poor Pip was so disappointed he could have cried. But just as he was about to let a little tear fall, he heard a voice far down the lane. It was calling HIM. "PIP! Pip! Where are you, Pip? Come along! It's time to go and meet the children from school."

All Pip's troubles vanished. He shot down the lane as fast as he could go, slithering over muddy places and splashing through puddles, the other dog that wasn't a dog but only an echo quite forgotten. His little master and mistress, his very best playmates, were coming home from school!

Jonathan John
Has A Lazy Day

Jonathan John had built himself a house on a hilly slope. It had a turf roof on which daisies and buttercups grew and a chimney made of stone. He built a shed for his cow and a sty for his pig. And then he asked the girl with the rosy cheeks and long yellow plaits to be his wife.

Gertrude made the little house snug inside. She cooked, she cleaned and she polished. She looked after the cow and the pig and she churned the butter. When the baby was born, she looked after him too. And every day, when the sun was overhead, she carried Jonathan's dinner to him in the field.

At the end of one summer's day, when the sun had made Jonathan feel hot and tired, and when his fingers were sore with weeding, he came home with an attack of the grumbles.

"You are very lucky, wife," he said to Gertrude.

"Why is that?" asked Gertrude. She was hot and tired too.

"Because you can stay at home all day and play with the baby," said Jonathan enviously.

"But I churn the butter, and look after the cow and the pig. I cook. I clean . . ."

Jonathan interrupted her. "You don't call that work, do you? Work is weeding and hoeing and raking. It seems very unfair to me that one of us should do all the work while the other does no work at all."

Jonathan grumbled and grumbled, and Gertrude decided that he would have to be taught a lesson before he turned the milk sour!

"Let's change places, just for one day," she said. "Tomorrow I will work in the field and you can stay at home."

Jonathan was quick to agree. Now Gertrude would find out for herself how hard he worked and how unfair it all was.

Next morning, Gertrude gave him a long list of instructions . . . don't wake the baby, boil the porridge, churn the butter, take the cow to pasture, don't let the pig escape from the sty, bring me my dinner . . . and then she went to the field.

"What a lazy day I am going to have," said Jonathan. As soon as Gertrude had gone, he stretched himself in a chair and went to sleep. He woke after an hour and began to churn the butter. Churning soon made his arm ache. It made him thirsty too.

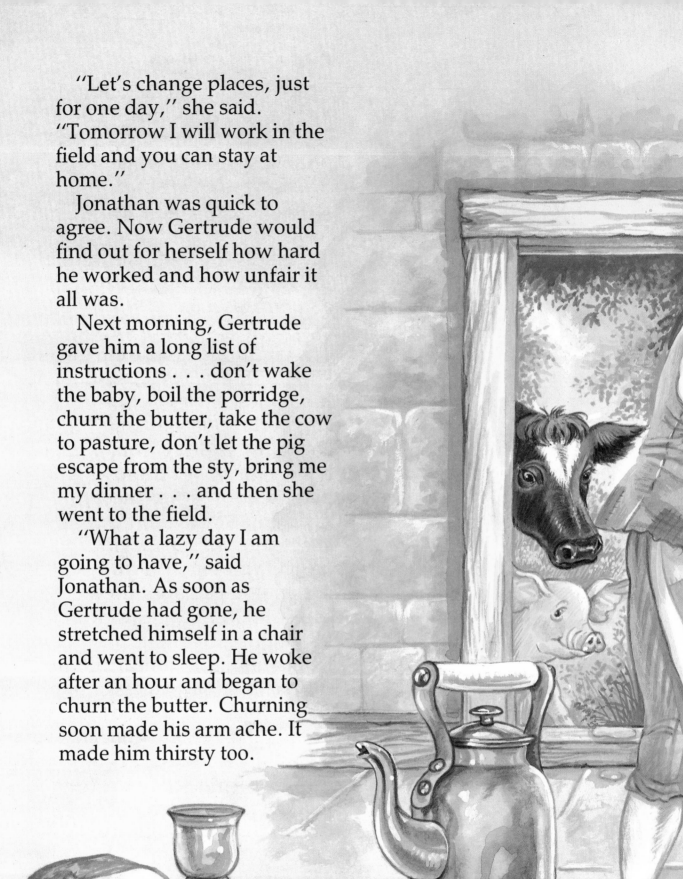

"I'll go down to the cellar and get myself a drink," he said. He was filling a jug from one of the barrels, when he heard the sound of pattering footsteps in the room above. "That sounds like the pig . . ." he said. He left the jug to finish filling from the barrel and ran upstairs.

What a sight met his eyes. The pig had escaped from the sty and had come indoors. It had knocked over the butter churn and was pattering about in a pool of half-made butter. What a mess those piggy footprints had made!

"Shoo . . . shoo . . !" shouted Jonathan, making more mess with his feet. He picked up a stool and threw it at the pig, and the pig ran squealing through the door. By the time he had cleaned up that mess, and the mess in the cellar, because of course the jug had overflowed while he was chasing the pig back to the sty, it was too late to take the cow to pasture.

"I'll put her on the roof," he said. "She can't come to any harm up there and she will find plenty to eat."

He led the cow up the hilly slope beside the house and pushed her onto the roof. She didn't like it very much. He tied a rope round her middle and dropped the long end down the chimney.

When he got back indoors, he tied the rope round his own waist. Now the cow couldn't possibly stray without him knowing.

"How much cleverer I am than Gertrude," he said. "Fancy walking the cow all the way to pasture, as she does, when there is grass growing on the roof."

He put the porridge pot on the fire, checked that the baby was still asleep, which he was, in spite of all the noise that had been going on, and sat down. He was surprised how tired he felt and it wasn't long before he was snoring. He woke very suddenly and was astonished to find himself half-way up the chimney, with no idea of how he had got there.

The answer was really simple. The cow wasn't used to grazing in such a small space, or one so high up. She had got too close to the edge of the roof and had fallen off. The rope saved her, but now she was dangling in mid-air, half-way between the roof and the ground! Because Jonathan and the cow were tied to different ends of the same rope, when the cow went DOWN, Jonathan couldn't do anything else but go UP. And that was how they stayed until Gertrude came home.

"Oh you poor cow," she cried when she saw the cow dangling in the air. She quickly cut the rope and the cow dropped to the ground with a grateful moo. There was a cry and a splash from within the house.

"Oh you poor man," laughed Gertrude as she helped Jonathan out of the porridge pot, for of course as soon as Gertrude cut the rope to release the cow, there was only one way Jonathan could go, and that was DOWN. He fell straight into the porridge pot! What a good thing it was that the fire had gone out and the porridge was cold.

"Tomorrow," said Jonathan, when Gertrude had washed the porridge from his face and kissed the end of his nose, "I will go to the field. You can stay at home. Too many things go wrong when I stay at home."

The Magic Pot

Once upon a time, there was a girl who lived with her mother in a tiny house on the outskirts of a small town. They were very poor and sometimes they were very hungry. They often had nothing to eat at all.

One day, when the girl was out in the woods searching for mushrooms and blackberries, she met an old woman who was carrying an empty iron pot.

"Take it," said the old woman putting the pot into her hands. "When you are hungry, say to it 'Little pot boil'. When you have enough, say, 'Little pot stop'."

The girl thought it very strange, but she took the pot home and told her mother what the old woman had said.

"Put it on the table, say the words, and we will see what happens," said her mother.

"Little pot boil," said the girl. Hardly were the words spoken than the pot began to bubble and hiss, and steam began to rise from it.

"It's filling up," gasped the girl.

"It's truly a magic pot," said her mother. "Stop it before it overflows."

"Little pot stop," said the girl. The bubbling and hissing stopped at once. "What a delicious smell," said the girl.

"That looks and smells very like porridge to me," said her mother. "Bring two plates and two spoons and we will taste it."

It was the sweetest, creamiest, nicest porridge either of them had ever tasted. And with a magic porridge pot like that at their command, their days of being hungry were over. It didn't matter how much porridge they ate, there was always some more to be had at the command 'Little pot boil'.

One day, when the girl was out, her mother set the pot on the table, and said, "Little pot boil". The bubbling began, the steam began to rise, the delicious smell of porridge began to fill the room. The sweet, creamy porridge reached the brim of the pot. The girl's mother opened her mouth to say the words to stop it and found she couldn't remember them. All she could think to say was, "Um er . . . that's enough". A tiny trickle of porridge began to run down the OUTSIDE of the porridge pot. The pot had never done that before. "Stop . . . stop . . ." she shouted in a panic. "I don't want any more . . . stop filling up . . . go away . . ." The harder she tried to remember the right words the worse it became.

The pot bubbled and bubbled. The trickle of porridge became a stream. It spread across the table and fell in a sticky cascade to the floor.

"Whatever shall I do?" she wailed as she climbed onto a chair. "Please . . . please . . . please stop . . . please pot!"

The pool of porridge spread to the door and ran out into the street.

"Stop! . . Stop! . ." she shouted. "Come back porridge . . . get back into the pot . . . please stop! . ." The porridge pot took no notice. It would only stop when it was given the right command. But what WAS the right command?

The sweet creamy porridge began to behave like an overflowing river. It ran on and on along the streets, into the houses and the dog kennels. It filled up the fish ponds and the drains.

"What's happening?" shouted the citizens of the town as they took off their shoes and waded through the sticky mess.

"It's the pot . . . it won't stop," cried the girl's mother.

The citizens began to shout commands then. The dogs began to bark and the cats began to miaow.

"Stop making porridge before we all drown . . . Stop! . . Stop! . ."

The girl was visiting at the far edge of the town. She heard the commotion and looked out of the window to see what the noise was about. As soon as she saw the rivers of porridge oozing through the streets she guessed at once what had happened. She ran home as fast as the sticky porridge would let her.

"Do something, do something quickly!" urged the townsfolk. When she got home her mother was still shouting commands at the pot. "Stop cooking . . . stop bubbling . . . Stop! . . Stop! . ."

"Little pot stop!" said the girl. THAT was the right command and the pot DID stop. Instantly.

"I'll only use the pot when you are here in future," said her mother. "I don't want that to happen again."

Neither did anyone else. It took ages to clean up the town and no one wants to do that kind of sticky job twice.

59

The Yellow Paint Pot

One afternoon, when Billy Green was walking along the lane, he found a pot of paint and a paint brush. The paint pot was standing on a post and the brush was lying across the top of the pot with paint dripping from its bristles. It looked as though someone had just put it down. Billy looked up the lane and down the lane. He could see no one at all.

"I know paint pots don't grow on posts," said Billy. "Someone must have put it there. Someone ought to keep an eye on it . . . just in case it falls off the post . . . or a bird knocks it over . . . or something." Any excuse was good enough to stand around and wait for the owner of the pot to come back. Whoever he was, perhaps he would let Billy paint a thing or two.

He waited two minutes. He waited five minutes. He waited ten minutes. The longer he waited the more his fingers itched to dip the brush into the paint. The paint was yellow, the colour of buttercups. It was thick, and oozy, like sticky custard.

Billy picked up the brush, not really meaning to dip it into the pot, but dip it he did. With the brush in his hand and full of yellow paint, he looked round for something to spread it on. All he could see was grass and flowers. Surely there was something he could paint. He looked down at his feet.

He thought how nice his shoes would look if they had yellow laces. Flick . . . swish . . . went the brush. The brush was wide and the shoelace narrow. Instead of a yellow lace in a brown shoe, Billy had a yellow lace in a yellow shoe!

"I'd better paint the other one to match," he gasped.

He didn't see the little man standing on the rim of the paint pot shaking his fist. He wouldn't have believed his eyes if he had. The little man was only ten centimetres tall. He was a buttercup painter. The paint pot belonged to him, and buttercup painters don't like little boys dabbling in their paint.

"Paint . . . brush . . . paint . . !" he bellowed as loudly as a foghorn on a foggy night.

Billy jumped twelve centimetres in the air when the voice boomed in his ear. He didn't have time to look around to see who the voice belonged to, because as his feet touched down again, the brush dipped itself into the paint pot and began to paint.

"Oh . . . oh . . ." squealed Billy. He tried to drop the brush. He couldn't. It was stuck to his hand. His fingers were curled round the handle as though they had been carved from the same piece of wood. In and out of the pot the brush went. In and out. Where the brush went, Billy's hand went, and where Billy's hand went the rest of him followed. One moment he was stretched like a giraffe, painting leaves on the trees, the next moment he was on his knees painting faces on the stones.

"What are you doing with my paint?" boomed the voice again.

"Nothing . . . I'm doing nothing at all," cried Billy, dizzily twirling round and round a tree as the brush painted a spiralling yellow stripe round its trunk. "It's not me, it's the brush."

"Nonsense, the brush is in YOUR hand," boomed the voice.

"But it won't let me put it down," cried Billy. He tried to shake his hand free, whereupon the brush shook HIM until he felt as wobbly as a jelly. All the time the brush shook it sprayed the air with blips of yellow paint, every one of which, in a most curious round-about way, landed somewhere on Billy.

"Oh . . . oh . . ." cried Billy. He was all spotty as though he had a bad dose of yellow measles!

"Shouldn't touch things that don't belong to you," boomed the voice.

"I won't . . . I won't . . . ever again," cried Billy. And he really meant what he said.

"Drop him, brush," ordered the little man as though he was talking to his pet dog.

The brush 'dropped' Billy as though he was an old slipper and began quietly painting a patch of buttercups in the grass, with no hand holding it at all.

Billy fled down the lane as though a swarm of bees was after him. Somewhere on the way he lost his yellow spots and his yellow shoe and so no one believed him when he explained about the magic paint brush. HE knew he hadn't been dreaming and what is more, he never again touched something that did not belong to him.

The King Of Birds

Once, long ago, the King of Birds lived with his subjects in the hilly highlands of Burma. One day, one of his subjects flew down to the flat lowlands. When he returned he called the other birds together.

"Today I have seen a marvellous thing," he said. "In the lowlands there are fields full of seeds just waiting to be eaten. It is foolish to spend so much time searching for food in the hills when it is waiting to be picked up in the fields."

"Let's all fly to the lowlands," twittered the birds in great excitement.

"Stay here, in the highlands, where you are safe," said the King of Birds, who was King because he was wise. "There will be men guarding the fields. You will be captured."

But the birds were so excited they wouldn't listen to his wise counsel. "We will fly in a flock," they said. "There is always safety in numbers."

Nothing the King said would make them change their minds and off they flew. When they reached the rice fields, they swooped down with a deafening chorus of chirps and cheeps and began to eat as fast as they could. "The King was wrong and we were right," they said, between mouthfuls.

But how wrong THEY were and how RIGHT the King was. The men who had planted the rice needed it for their families and they were determined the birds should not have it. They had prepared a trap. The birds had never seen a net before.

They did not know that a simple looking thing could be so dangerous.

Suddenly there was a shout. Men and boys jumped from hiding places in the field and sprang the net. The birds were captured. Every single one. They fluttered and they struggled but the net was strong and held them tightly.

"The King was right and WE were wrong," they said sadly.

Up in the highlands, the King was scanning the sky anxiously. His subjects had been gone a long time. Too long. Something must have happened. He decided to go to the lowlands himself.

"It's the King," chatted the birds when they saw him. "It's the King . . . oh please help us."

The King of Birds, who was King not only because he was wise, but because he was kind as well, said, "I can only help you if you do exactly as I tell you."

"We will . . . we will . . ." twittered the birds eagerly.

When the King of Birds was sure everyone was listening, he said, "When I give the signal you must all beat your wings at the same time and rise into the sky together."

"We are ready . . . we are ready . . ." twittered the birds.

"NOW!" commanded the King of Birds, who was King not only because he was kind and wise, but because he could command as well. Up flew the birds. UP UP UP in a great fluttering cloud. As they rose into the sky, the net that surrounded them on all sides, rose into the air with them. They were still trapped.

"Fly! Fly! Fly! Follow me home to the highlands," ordered the King of Birds as his subjects began to panic.

What a strange sight it was
to see a net full of birds flying
across the sky. They reached
the highlands safely. But they
were still not free.

"Are we to stay in this net
forever?" they asked one
another.

"I will get help," said the
King of Birds. He called upon
his friend the mouse. "Please
come at once," he said.

"What can a tiny mouse do against such a big net?" asked
the birds sadly when they saw the tiny, scampering creature
sniffing round the edge of the net. The mouse scampered
away and they saw a chance of escape, even if it was small,
disappear.

"Please come back . . . we didn't mean to offend you," they
chirped. "The King was right before. Maybe he is right again.
Maybe you CAN help us."

They had no reason to worry. The mouse had gone to fetch his relations. What one mouse can do in an hour, a dozen mice can do in a minute. What did they do? They nibbled and gnawed at the strands of the net. One by one the strands snapped. Soon there was a hole large enough for even the largest bird to slip through without damaging his tail feathers.

One by one they soared into the sky and spread their wings. ''The King was right,'' they sang. ''The King was right.''

The net lay empty and forgotten on the ground.

How good it was to be free. How lucky the birds were to have a King who was kind enough to forgive their foolishness and wise enough to find an answer to a problem that seemed to have no solution.

71

A Singing Lesson

Fred Frog had a deep baritone voice and he liked to sing.

"Please sing me a song, Fred," Freda Frog would say. Fred would first find a place to sit and then he would wobble his chin and serenade her with the croakiest of croaks.

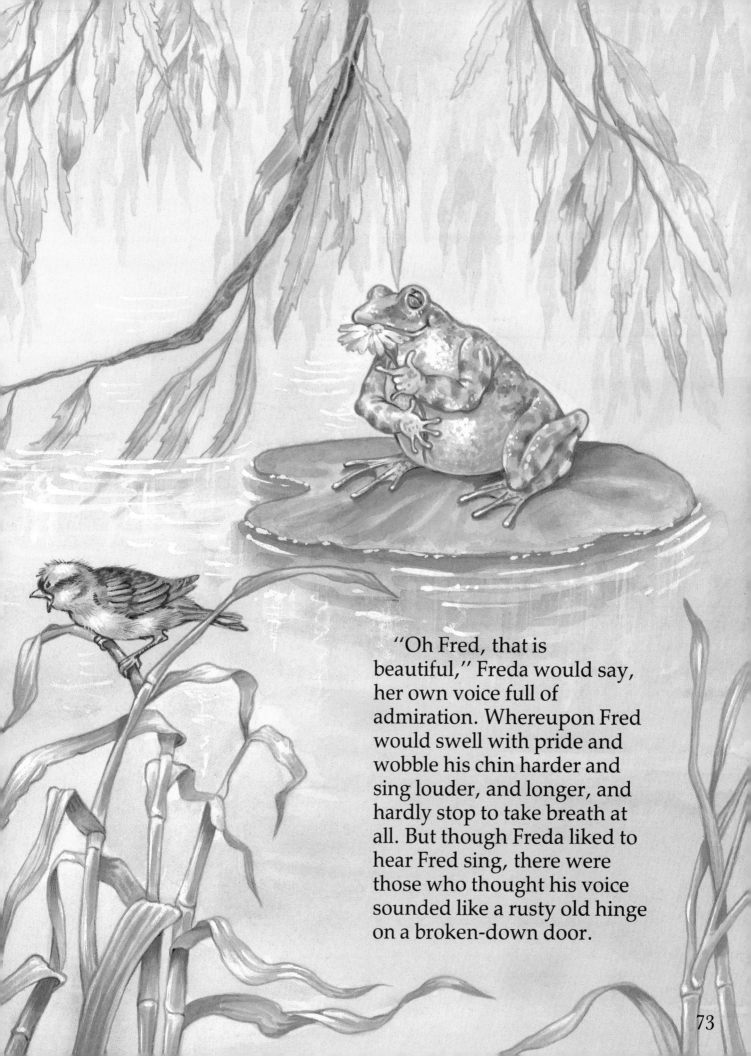

"Oh Fred, that is beautiful," Freda would say, her own voice full of admiration. Whereupon Fred would swell with pride and wobble his chin harder and sing louder, and longer, and hardly stop to take breath at all. But though Freda liked to hear Fred sing, there were those who thought his voice sounded like a rusty old hinge on a broken-down door.

One day, when Fred was singing, Reggie Reed-Warbler called: "Hey Fred, where's your oil can?"

"I should take some singing lessons if I were you," called Wally Wagtail.

"We can't hear OURSELVES sing with that racket going on," called the curlews.

"You sound like a cornflake with a sore throat," said the meadow-pipit.

The underneath part of Fred's chin stopped wobbling and his lip started to wobble instead. His feelings were hurt.

"Take no notice," said Freda. "They only say those things because they are jealous of your beautiful voice."

"Jealous of HIS voice," laughed the birds. "When we have such beautiful voices of our own? Don't be silly . . . now boys, let's show those frogs what real singing is all about."

The birds whistled and sang and filled the sky and the wind with the beautiful sounds that only birds can make. Poor Fred. A tear rolled down his cheek. He slid noiselessly into the water and hid in the mud on the bottom of the pond.

"Please don't cry," said Freda as she sidled into the mud beside him. "Your voice is the most beautiful voice in the world to me."

"If only I could sing like a bird," sighed Fred. "If only I could whistle and trill." And no matter what Freda said, Fred would not come out of the mud.

"Where's Fred?" asked Reggie Reed-Warbler next morning.

"You have hurt his feelings because you laughed at him," said Freda. "You have made him ashamed of his own voice and now he wishes he could sing like you."

Reggie Reed-Warbler thought for a moment. The birds hadn't meant to be unkind to Fred. "If he wants to sing like a bird, then we will teach him," he said. "Go and fetch him, Freda."

Freda really did prefer Fred's voice the way it was, but she went and got him all the same because she knew that was what Fred would have wanted. Fred came up and sat beside her on a lily-pad and waited for his lesson to begin. The birds sat in the reeds facing him.

"This shouldn't take long," said Reggie.

Fred concentrated very hard. He really did. First Reggie showed him how to sing. Then Wally tried. And then all the other birds tried. Still Fred's voice did nothing but croak and creak and groan.

"No . . . no . . . Not like that," said Reggie for the hundredth time as yet another peculiar squeaky croak came from Fred's throat.

"I'm trying . . . I really am," said Fred.

"He is . . ." said Freda. "I can tell."

"You're being stubborn," shouted Reggie at last. "You don't want to sing like a bird."

"But I do . . . I do . . ." sobbed Fred. His poor green face looked back at him from the water. His tears plopped like pebbles and made his reflection disappear.

Tired and exasperated though the birds were, they began to feel sorry for him.

"Do cheer up," they said. "It's not your fault you can't sing like a bird."

It was then that Freda had an idea. "I don't suppose," she said, "that birds can croak like frogs either."

Fred's head jerked up and his tears stopped.

"Of course they can," said Reggie.

"Let's hear you then," said Freda.

The birds tried, they really did, but the sounds that came from their throats as they tried to croak like frogs were as strange as the sounds that came from Fred's throat when he tried to sing like a bird.

"I must admit," said Reggie, "that Fred is better at croaking than we are."

"I told you he had a beautiful voice," said Freda.

"I suppose he has, for a frog," admitted Reggie.

And that was how it ended, for after all, who wants to listen to a bird who croaks like a frog, or a frog who sings like a bird. A frog is a frog and a bird is a bird. Frogs croak, birds whistle, and that's the way it should be.

Humpty Dumpty

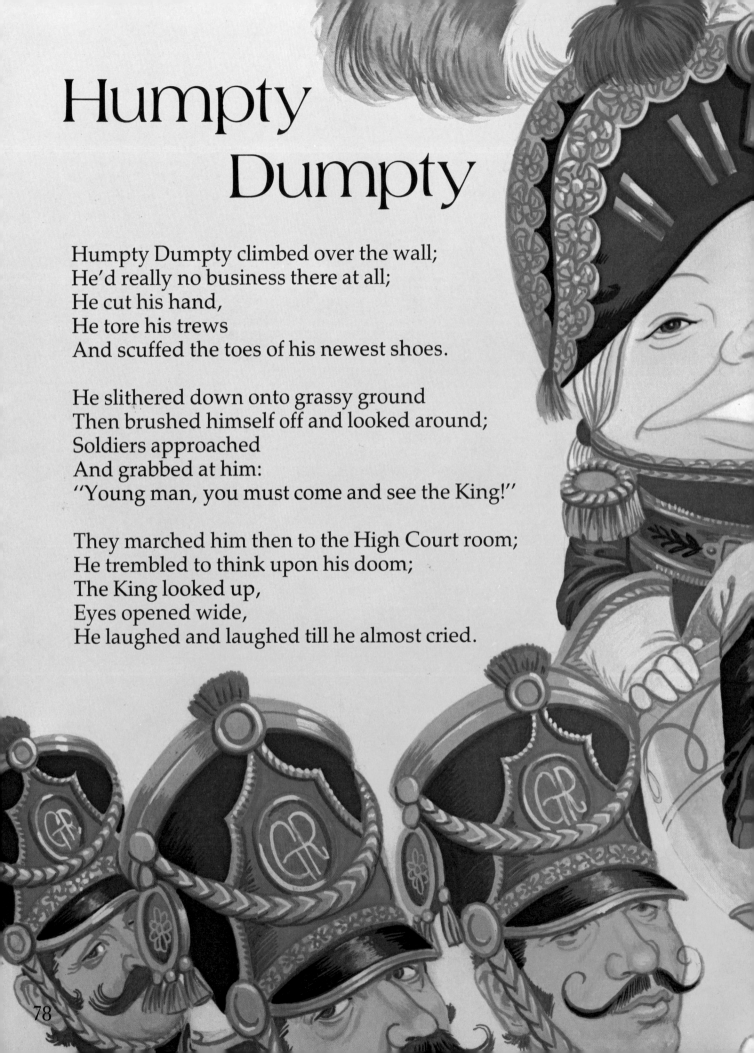

Humpty Dumpty climbed over the wall;
He'd really no business there at all;
He cut his hand,
He tore his trews
And scuffed the toes of his newest shoes.

He slithered down onto grassy ground
Then brushed himself off and looked around;
Soldiers approached
And grabbed at him:
"Young man, you must come and see the King!"

They marched him then to the High Court room;
He trembled to think upon his doom;
The King looked up,
Eyes opened wide,
He laughed and laughed till he almost cried.

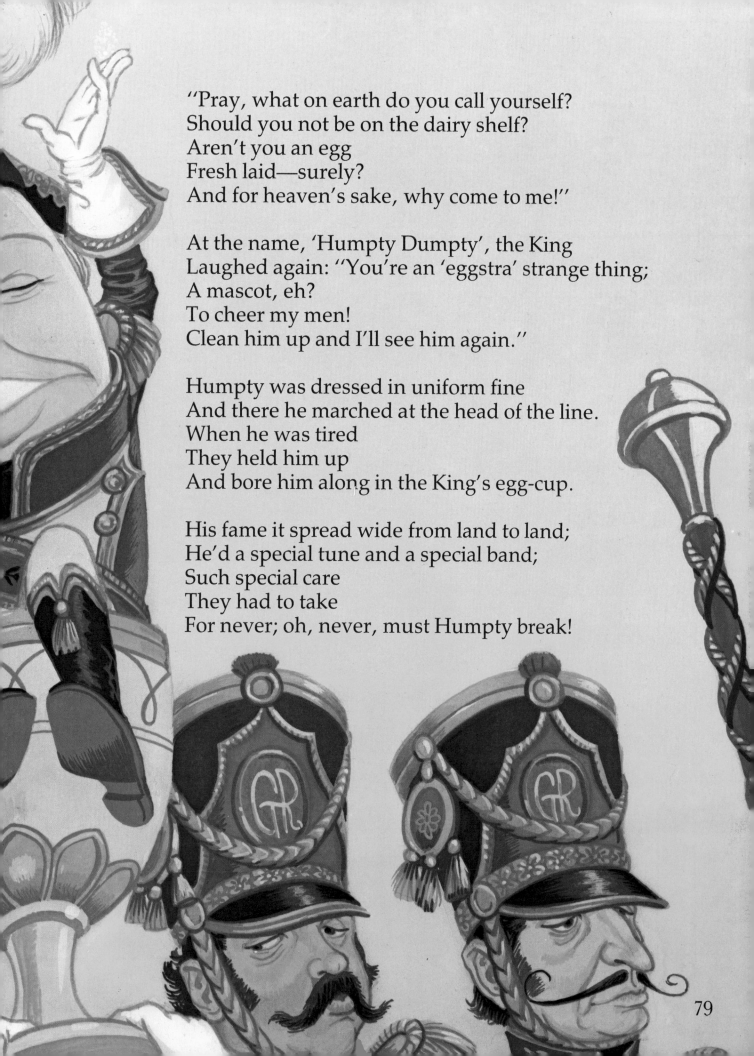

"Pray, what on earth do you call yourself?
Should you not be on the dairy shelf?
Aren't you an egg
Fresh laid—surely?
And for heaven's sake, why come to me!"

At the name, 'Humpty Dumpty', the King
Laughed again: "You're an 'eggstra' strange thing;
A mascot, eh?
To cheer my men!
Clean him up and I'll see him again."

Humpty was dressed in uniform fine
And there he marched at the head of the line.
When he was tired
They held him up
And bore him along in the King's egg-cup.

His fame it spread wide from land to land;
He'd a special tune and a special band;
Such special care
They had to take
For never; oh, never, must Humpty break!

Bedtime

The evening is coming,
The sun sinks to rest;
The rooks are all flying
Straight home to the nest,
"Caw!" says the rook, as he flies overhead,
"It's time little people were going to bed!"

The flowers are closing;
The daisy's asleep,
The primrose is buried
In slumber so deep.
Shut up for the night is the pimpernel red;
It's time little people were going to bed!

The butterfly drowsy,
Has folded its wings;
The bees are returning,
No more the birds sing.
Their labour is over, their nestlings are fed;
It's time little people were going to bed!